the ghost downstairs

the ghost downstairs

Leon Garfield

Illustrated by Antony Maitland

Kestrel Books

KESTREL BOOKS
Published by Penguin Books Ltd
Harmondsworth, Middlesex, England

Copyright © 1972 by Leon Garfield
Illustrations Copyright © 1972
by Antony Maitland

First published 1972 under the
Longman Young Books imprint
Second impression 1973
Third impression 1975
Fourth impression 1977

ISBN 0 7226 5094 9

Printed in Great Britain by
Lowe & Brydone Printers Limited, Thetford, Norfolk

To Philippa Christie

part one

1 Two devils lived in Mr Fast: envy and loneliness. Together they gnawed at him; drained the colour from
his face, the lustre from his eyes and the charity from
his heart.

By day he worked as a clerk in a solicitor's office in
Lamb's Court, where he followed his bland-faced employer
through every grimy secret passage in the rusty chainwork
of the law. Diligently he mastered each twist and turn until
he came to be regarded—in the trade—as a remarkably
astute young man; "one who had his head screwed on
right", and was capable of drawing up a Contract or an
Agreement like a maze in which careless fools might wander
till they died. Nor was he done with them then—as many a
beneficiary found to his cost. Wills were child's play to
Mr Fast—though God help the child who played thus.

At night, neatly dressed in black, with a short round hat
that resembled the stopper of an ink bottle, he returned to

Highbury New Park where he had rooms on the ground floor of Number Fourteen. Here, in his respectable living-room that always smelled of camphor, he would sit for hours together surrounded by items of heavy mahogany furniture and two tomb-like armchairs—all of which had been picked up, so to speak, at sales of Effects at the houses of deceased clients. So strong indeed was the air of bereavement that the very sideboard and table, weighty though they were, seemed unnaturally still—as if they'd lately died and left themselves to Mr Fast in their wills.

Sometimes he'd take a small glass of port; and then the two devils inside him would get to work and the clerk would dream his dreams. He would dream of owning the whole house, of being rich and powerful, of employing his employer and lording it over a streetful of friends whose chief occupation would be to dance attendance on him of an evening and especially of a week-end. Truly, if Mr Fast's dreams ever contrived to survive the grave and haunt the high-class neighbourhood in which he pinched and scraped to live, they would have made a frightful ghost indeed—a spectre to frighten even God; a thin, gibbering misery in a shroud of business suiting, with fingers like quill pens, scratching arithmetic on moonbeams and prices on children's eyes.

Lately, his dreams had acquired an even sharper edge. They concerned an old man who lived in the basement—a shabby, disgusting old man by the name of Fishbane. He'd arrived on the very day that old Dr Herz—who'd perished rather abruptly one midnight—had been buried.

Mr Fast had watched through the window while the old doctor, neatly coffined, had been hoisted up the area steps and into the glass-sided hearse where he lay, under a rich crust of chrysanthemums, like an expensive cake in the window of Fortnum and Mason's. When the funeral moved off, Mr Fast had nipped down to the basement to see if anything had been overlooked. He'd actually been in the shabby living-room, his hand on the sideboard drawer, when Mr Fishbane had appeared.

Of course, there'd been a little awkwardness, but Mr Fast was peculiarly adept at wriggling out sideways and explaining anything to anybody's satisfaction. Mr Fishbane hadn't seemed at all put out and Mr Fast thankfully withdrew to his own apartment from where he watched the old man unloading sacks, bundles and two enormous saucepans from a handcart in the street outside.

Considering his age, he seemed remarkably spry going up and down the area steps; and with his festoonery of ancient black garments that hung about him like decrepit wings, and his creased old neck that stretched forward under his burdens, he resembled a very shabby vulture that, for reasons of health and vanity, had taken to wearing a broad-brimmed hat.

Understandably, Mr Fast was not altogether delighted to have such a neighbour. Highbury New Park had always been considered a better class of district and he, Mr Fast, had made real sacrifices to live there. Now came Mr Fishbane and there was no doubt he brought the tone down. One might almost say there was a strong whiff of the ghetto about him. And that wasn't the only whiff, either.

Old Dr Herz in his time had produced some pretty strong smells in the basement; but they turned out to have been perfumes beside Mr Fishbane's. For two days after he moved in he'd burned sulphur till the whole house reeked of it, so as not to catch whatever had carried the doctor off. Then he boiled beetroots, day and night, it seemed, for soup. To Mr Fast's sensitive nose, the stench was unbearable, so he bought more and more camphor balls which he stuffed behind the cushions of his chairs, beneath his pillow and under the turkey carpet where he occasionally trod on them with a noise like cracking bones. But do what he might, there was no overpowering the beetroot soup, and the general effect, in Mr Fast's apartment, was of some large, invisible banquet that was steadily going off.

Nonetheless, though the clerk never actually spoke to Mr Fishbane if he chanced to pass him in the street, he was careful not to show that he strongly objected to the old man

and despised his meagre appearance from the bottom of his soul.

The reason for this caution was that there was something about Mr Fishbane that suggested property. Mr Fast couldn't quite put his finger on it, but somehow the shrewd solicitor's clerk smelled property. Naturally he attempted to make inquiries but, try as he might, he was unable to discover anything. The name "Fishbane" appeared on no Lists and had been heard of in no Proceedings. So far as the Law and the City were concerned, Mr Fishbane didn't exist and the clerk was on the point of dismissing his suspicions as being imagination, when an unusual thing happened to restore his faith in them.

Mr Fishbane turned up at the stone-setting ceremony for Dr Herz—which Mr Fast also attended as it was on a Sunday and not raining. But what a changed Mr Fishbane it was! The old man had looked really respectable in a black frock coat, striped trousers and a tall silk hat that perched on his filthy tangle of yellow-grey hair like a chimney pot on thatch.

"A Beneficiary!" thought Mr Fast instantly; and wondered how much.

After the ceremony he made a point of button-holing his interesting neighbour; but Mr Fishbane seemed reluctant to leave the graveside. He kept blinking rheumily at the slab of shiny speckled marble on which was advertised: "Dr Otto Herz; Professor of Natural Science at Wittenburg and Aberdeen. Taken suddenly in the midst of his labours, aged seventy."

"Poor soul," murmured Mr Fishbane, bowing his head so that Mr Fast feared his hat would fall off and land among the flowers.

"Oh, I don't know," said Mr Fast. "I suppose he must have been quite well off. That marble must have cost a pretty penny."

Mr Fishbane looked up and fixed the clerk with so deep and melancholy a gaze that Mr Fast couldn't help supposing the old man to be thinking of his own decease—which, in the course of nature, was unlikely to be far off. Really, he might pop off anytime, thought the clerk, shrewdly eyeing the old gentleman's unwholesome complexion.

Once this thought was in his mind, there was no getting it out again—not that Mr Fast tried to evict it. Indeed it was a welcome tenant and got on famously with the two devils that lived there. In a manner of speaking, all three of them held parties in his head and dined off Mr Fishbane's estate.

The clerk's imagination, liberated nightly from the twisting and turning and screwing down of his daily labours, spread its wings and soared in the direction he'd always supposed to be up.

An eccentric millionaire; that's what the old man might be. One was always hearing about them, going about in rags and tatters with fortunes sewn in their underwear. Thank God he'd never insulted him! By all accounts, such crazy old gentlemen had powerful memories. They were always leaving thousands to newspaper boys and crossing sweepers who'd tipped their hats and said "good morning" to them as they'd shuffled past each day until they came at last to Probate.

Such were Mr Fast's evening dreams as he sat in his tomb of an armchair, quite enveloped in the fumes of camphor and beetroot soup. By day, of course, he dismissed his fancies—even smiling at them into the privacy of his desk; but once in Highbury New Park, they came creeping back with a curiously increasing urgency.

Any silence in the basement immediately inspired him with the fear that Mr Fishbane had popped off before the clerk had had a chance to make his mark on him and ease himself into the old man's prosperous soul. He'd sit and gnaw his fingernails and clutch his bottle of port as if he'd wring its neck . . . until sounds from the basement reassured him and his dreams once more took wing.

But man—even a solicitor's clerk—cannot live on dreams alone. One day, towards the end of October, Mr Fast came back from Lamb's Court with a crystal decanter, wrapped up in newspaper, that he'd picked up at a sale of effects of a client who'd lately shot himself, preferring to be hammered in his coffin than hammered on 'Change.

Carefully he unwrapped his parcel, filled the decanter from his port bottle, and examined it with satisfaction. He liked such little refinements; they gave a polish to living. He sat down and stared into the crimson depths until he began to see himself twinkling away in the decanter's myriad facets—a whole world of peering, prying clerks, each in his own little sepulchre of glass.

Presently, with a slight shock, he became aware that the basement had been silent since he'd come in. He frowned and listened carefully; and all the other clerks seemed to put their ears to their sepulchre walls and listen with him. Not a sound. Perhaps the old man had gone out? He went to the window and peered into the dark area. A blade of yellow light fell across it. Alive or dead, Mr Fishbane was at home.

Mr Fast waited several minutes longer, listening acutely. The silence continued. The suspense was intolerable; Mr Fast was unable to think of anything but a dead millionaire under his very feet. Several times already he'd got up and gone to his door; and then he'd drawn back. At last he could bear it no longer; it was more than his flesh and blood could stand. He left his apartment and went outside. He pushed open the iron gate to the area steps. The hinges squealed and groaned. The clerk paused, shivering in the chilly, night air. Still no sound from the old man's home. He began to creep down the steps, imagining the old man lying like a sack on the floor, with a cashbox close at hand; when suddenly he was enveloped in yellow light. The basement door had opened.

"Good evening, Mr Fast," said Mr Fishbane. "I was wondering when you'd come down."

2 "Come in, young man, come inside," said Mr Fishbane, beaming in his matted beard; and Mr Fast, recovering from his shock, followed him into the basement.

"So good of you to call on an old man. And you with all your friends and engagements . . ."

There was not a trace of mockery in the old man's voice, yet his words struck shrewdly at Mr Fast's heart. The clerk's eyes misted briefly at the unaccustomed pain; then he said, "Yes . . . yes . . ." in as off-hand a tone as he could manage.

It turned out that Mr Fishbane was just going to have

supper, but Mr Fast was very welcome to a drop of soup—
"And port wine for afters, I see," added the old man, rub-
bing his hands together. "A kind thought, young man.
I appreciate that!"

With a start, Mr Fast realised his agitation had been so
great he'd come down still clutching his decanter. He
coughed, and peered round the dingy living room for signs
of secret wealth. The furniture was nothing to write home
about. It consisted of a sideboard, table and three chairs, all
of dismal age and ugliness, and, in front of the fire, a monstrous leather couch that seemed to have been thrashed raw
about the arms and back by some brute of an upholsterer
determined to break its spirit.

Certainly something had been broken in it, for when Mr
Fast seated himself while the old man was busy in the kitchen,
he went down a long way before meeting with any resist-
ance. On the credit side however were a fine pair of silver
candlesticks on the mantelpiece and an oil painting of what
appeared to be a religious subject depicting a scene of vague
but unpleasant torment. It was so dim and depressing that
Mr Fast wouldn't have been surprised to learn that it was
worth a fortune. One was always hearing of such things
turning up in basements up and down the country.

"Sentimental value only," said Mr Fishbane, coming in
with a steaming saucepan that made its own weather in the
room and observing the clerk's interest in the picture.

He set the saucepan on the table and ladled the blood-red
liquid into two cracked china cups. "Not very refined,
young man, but nourishing."

He crumbled a biscuit into his soup and sucked away at it.
Mr Fast, half choked by the aroma, bravely followed suit.
To his surprise, the taste was quite pleasant; it was sweetish
and creamy and seemed to have been laced with wine. He
had three cups of it, by which time he was thoroughly at his
ease. He had discovered Mr Fishbane had been in the manu-
facturing line but was now retired.

"So I do a little in Insurance; just trifles here and there, to keep myself going," said the old man, with a tinge of regret.

"There's money in Insurance," said Mr Fast shrewdly.

"It's a living. But I do it more for the occupation rather than the profit, young man."

There's money here all right, thought the clerk with satisfaction. More for the occupation than the profit indeed! He must be as rich as the Pope.

"A glass of port, Mr Fishbane?"

"Just a drop, young man. My old head won't stand very much these days."

He produced two glasses and Mr Fast laughingly filled them both to the brim. They drank to better days, cheerful nights and mud in one another's eyes—and there was no doubt the old man was rapidly affected. He grew quite sentimental and affectionate. Several times he laid his hand on the clerk's obliging shoulder and insisted on calling him "sonny" and "Dennis". For a moment the clerk was honestly at a loss and even looked round to see who "Dennis" might be. Then he realised it was his own Christian name and was even on the card outside his door; no one had called him by it for twenty years or more.

The conversation ranged far and wide, though it was the clerk who did most of the talking. He told one or two legal jokes that were all the rage about the Courts, but Mr Fishbane didn't seem to get the hang of them; so Mr Fast sang the chorus of a drinking song which seemed to please him much better. He wagged his smelly old head indulgently back and forth, sometimes joining in with a wobbly hum.

I'm making quite a hit with him, thought the clerk with pride. It pays to be sociable. And the port was a real stroke of genius. Though Mr Fishbane had drunk scarcely half a glass to Mr Fast's four or five, there was no doubt who had his wits most about him. The clerk smiled to himself and reflected that he could cut stars out of the old man's beard without his noticing. He sang another little song—rather a spicy one—and peered at the decanter, expecting to see his intoxicated companion imprisoned in the glittering facets. But the light was such that he saw only his myriad selves, still peering and prying at a million glass walls as if beyond them there was something more than just another prying clerk.

He was growing dizzy; he knew it. It was the heat in the room. He must get a hold on himself and turn the conversation to bring the old man into line. He must get him talking about money.

"I'd like to do something for you, Dennis," said Mr Fishbane, quite out of the blue. The clerk could scarcely believe his ears. Had he such strength of mind that his secret wishes had actually forced the old man's thoughts?

"If you wouldn't be offended, I'd like to give you something."

Amazing! Exactly what the clerk had had in mind! He was almost frightened by this demonstration of his own power.

"What are your dreams, sonny? What is it you long for? Tell old Fishbane and maybe old Fishbane can help."

The clerk smiled and shook his head roguishly. How drunk was the old man? How much could Mr Fast rely on what he promised? That was the point—

"Why not try me, sonny?"

The clerk started. The old man's mind seemed close enough to be breathing down the neck of his own. It was quite uncanny.

"I hardly like to say, Mr Fishbane," said the clerk cautiously; and concentrated fiercely on willing the old man to make him an actual offer.

"Wouldn't you like to have done with loneliness and envy, Dennis?"

Damnation! The old fool had missed a turning and gone off into sentimental rubbish. If the clerk wasn't careful he'd end up with nothing more than salvation and a charity dinner.

"Now you come to mention it, Mr Fishbane, I've always wanted a bit of property."

"And the loneliness?"

"Property attracts friends, you know."

"You don't ask much, sonny."

I'll take all you can give, thought Mr Fast, stung by the condescension in the old man's words.

"Suppose, just suppose I could give you anything in the world, Dennis."

The clerk stared at him, wondering if the old man was having him on. A twinge of anger pinched his heart. Just let me know what you're worth, he thought sharply, then I'll know what to ask for!

"The riches of the world," murmured Mr Fishbane dreamily, "and all you ask is a little bit of property."

Who did the old man think he was? Mr Fast observed that the old man's glass was almost empty. He must be as drunk as a judge, sitting there in his filthy old clothes and offering anything in the world to a solicitor's clerk who'd dealt with more fortunes than he'd had hot dinners.

"Health, wealth and happiness," mumbled Mr Fishbane in a manner the clerk could only describe as fuddled.

"Ah yes, health is a great blessing," said Mr Fast, anxious to get it out of the way before the tipsy old fellow offered a bag of charcoal biscuits and called it a day. "But between you, me and this decanter, sir, I'd sooner be in prosperous circumstances with a touch of catarrh than be as fit as a fiddle and sleeping on the Embankment! First things first, Mr Fishbane—and devil take the hindmost, as they say!"

"Do they, sonny? I always fancied the devil would have been nearer to the foremost."

"I won't tangle with you on theology, Mr Fishbane," laughed the clerk. "I can see you're too well up in it."

Careful, careful. These crazy old millionaires often turn out to be religious maniacs, thought the clerk. Mustn't offend their beliefs. He glanced up towards the old man's painting with an air of respectfulness.

The detail in the picture seemed to stand out a little more clearly than it had at his first glance. It was one of those busy pictures, stuffed with crosses and a great many figures scampering over a glossy landscape like mice. Here and there he could see tiny bony bottoms, and he wondered why some of the figures were naked while the others were respectably dressed—and might, from the look of them, have been hurrying across Threadneedle street for some item of City news. It really was very queer; and as the firelight flickered and the gas mantle chuckled, the figures actually seemed to move. The naked ones were setting fire to the coat tails of the others, and there could be seen little bonfires, running, jumping and falling from the tops of high buildings. One in particular intrigued him. It was wearing a round black hat, a little like his own, and was capering down a hauntingly familiar street, its legs going like a pair of scissors and flaring from every limb.

An extraordinary chill pierced the clerk. He averted his eyes—then fearfully looked again. But the figure was lost in the general holocaust. It was impossible to pick it out and determine which of the tiny howling faces had looked so horribly like his own.

He was about to take another glass of port to fortify himself, when he wisely reflected that his imagination was already overheated. It was all the talk that was doing it. The clerk was really only at home with documents. Words needed to be pinned down on paper—like dead insects. Then one knew where one was. Give him a Deed, or a Lease or a Covenant, and he'd show the old man what was what. He'd have him tied up like a chicken.

"I wonder if you'd be interested in a Policy, Dennis," murmured the old man. "Just one of my own, you know."

The clerk could scarcely restrain a grin of triumph at this latest success of his thoughts. He nodded—and Mr Fishbane shuffled off out of the room.

Mr Fast rubbed his neat hands together in anticipation and smirked at his decanter; when once more he was chilled. The level of the port was substantially lowered. Stains and trickles of the wine adhered to the sides so that the gallery of entombed clerks seemed daubed and smeared with blood. And behind each and every one reared a gaunt, top-hatted figure in black. Uneasily he turned—then saw with relief that the dreadful figure was nothing more than Mr Fishbane's Sunday-go-a-burying hat and coat, hanging behind the door.

"Here it is, sonny," wheezed Mr Fishbane, returning with his Policy and a pen and ink. "Just you tell me what Benefit you have in mind, Dennis, and old Fishbane will do the rest. All you have to do is to sign—"

"Like a receipt?"

The old man shrugged his shoulders and the clerk took the document and scanned it with a professional eye. He smiled pityingly.

"Really, Mr Fishbane—it's lucky for you I'm in the Law. My dear sir, you don't protect yourself at all. It's too simple and, if I may say so, childlike. Any good lawyer could pick a dozen holes in it."

"And so could a rat," said the old man. He seemed a shade down-hearted that his Policy had been dismissed as incompetent. "What do you suggest, then, Dennis?"

"Well, sir—if, as I understand it, you wish to make a Deed of Gift, then it will have to be drawn up properly. If, on the other hand, you really intend to utter a Policy, then we must consider the Premium I would be required to pay. Then again, on the other hand—"

"How many hands have you, sonny?"

"A good solicitor needs two in front and one behind his back, Mr Fishbane!" chuckled the clerk, quoting his employer who was a noted wit. "But as I was saying, sir, if you intend some sort of Contract, then I must still pay something—quite nominal, of course—as my part of the bargain. Otherwise, I'm afraid, the Courts would throw it out. It's really all for your protection, sir."

Mr Fishbane nodded. "I like the idea of a bargain, Dennis. Let's make it a bargain between us. You have your heart's desire and I have—"

"A pound is the usual sum between friends," said the clerk eagerly.

"No money, I beg of you. I've more than I know what to do with."

"What else is there, sir?"

"What about your soul, Dennis?"

"My *what*?"

The clerk blinked. The old fool thought he was the devil! It was money for old rope—or, rather, old souls! But it was particularly important, the clerk realised, not to laugh outright. One had to humour the old man.

Mr Fishbane sat staring at him across the table. His expression was curiously pleading and humble, as if he was wondering—as well he might—if he'd said the right thing or whether he'd over-reached himself and lost a valued friend.

"Bless me!" said Mr Fast, with all the solemnity he could muster. "I do begin to suppose you must be the devil himself, sir! Bargains for souls, and all that. What an extraordinary thing to happen in Highbury New Park!"

He paused. The old gentleman looked quite affronted.

"Why should it be the devil who wants to give you something for nothing, sonny?"

"Not for nothing, Mr Fishbane. For my soul, you said."

"Ain't that nothing, Dennis?"

Now it was the clerk's turn to look offended. Although he'd never reckoned his soul to be a negotiable security, he'd always supposed he'd had one. The old man had as good as insulted him in a very private place.

"No offence, sonny. You draw up the Contract as you see fit. Take what you like and give what you like—as long as it's not money."

He fetched a sheet of clean paper and passed it to the clerk.

"It's not that I'd deny you my soul," murmured the clerk, beginning to scratch at the paper. He tried to sound off-hand. Now he came to think of it, to part with a soul, for someone in his situation, would be more comfortable

than parting with a pound. "It's just that it's difficult to describe it in a legal Contract. The Courts wouldn't like it, Mr Fishbane. They're sticklers for detail; and you can't be detailed about a soul. After all, what is it? How much does it weigh? Do you keep it on the public highway? Do you license it—or pay any tax on it? You see, Mr Fishbane, life is very complicated when you get down to brass tacks."

"Where do you keep your soul, Dennis?"

The clerk stuck his pen behind his ear and tried to look serious and thoughtful.

"Somewhere inside, I suppose."

"Then give me yourself—just a moment off the end of your life; no matter how short . . . just so long as I'll have you complete with your soul."

"Fixtures and fittings, eh?"

"Put it how you like."

"It's how the Courts like, sir. It's all for your protection, you understand."

He frowned. A moment off the end of his life. What a crazy Contract! He shook his head; and then, from sheer force of habit, he began to examine the notion and see how it might be satisfactorily framed. He began to consider the words and see how they might be twisted and looped and knotted to his own advantage. He took the pen from behind his ear and began to write in an elegant but tiny script. The words danced off his pen nib like scurrying ants. He looked up. "You said a moment, sir. I'm afraid one must be more exact than that. A moment might be anything. A Judge would laugh it out of Court, you know."

"We mustn't have it laughed out of Court," said Mr Fishbane anxiously.

"Never mind, sir. I'll put in an actual span from the end of my life. I'll tie it up legally. Now—as for the sum of money you had in mind—"

"The sum of money *you* had in mind," said the old man; rather reproachfully, the clerk thought. "I talked of the riches of the world. It was you who mentioned money, Dennis."

"The riches of the world are generally expressed in terms of money," said Mr Fast, a shade snappishly. "It's only what the Courts expect, sir," he went on, relenting into a smile. "There's nothing vague about money. One knows where one is. Whether it's a hundred or a thousand or a million, Mr Fishbane, it represents what you and I would call the riches of the world—heart's desire—happiness and all that sort of thing that simply can't be pinned down in any other way."

"Then make it a million, sonny."

"I beg your pardon, sir?"

"A million, Dennis."

"Pounds?"

"Or guineas. I won't haggle."

The clerk had put down his pen. He stared at the old man with all the penetration he could command. The offer was so outrageous it was almost insulting. Did the old fool take him for a child? He began to be very angry.

"What's the matter, sonny? Don't you think I can afford it?"

The clerk could not bring himself to say "no", so the old man went on: "Didn't you say you thought I was the devil, Dennis?"

Helplessly the clerk nodded. He had indeed made such a statement.

"Then why not believe in the million? The devil ain't poor, sonny. Put down the million."

The clerk swallowed hard. He wrote down "a million pounds" in somewhat larger letters than usual. It looked like a madman's dream. He glared across the table. The old man was still perfectly serious. Not the ghost of a smile flickered in his faded eyes nor shivered the forests of his beard.

My God! thought Mr Fast wildly; what if he *is* the devil? He bit his lip. The devil in a better class district like Highbury New Park? What a ridiculous notion. The port was going to his head. He's nothing but an old madman with a mint of money and the sooner he's parted from it the better for all concerned.

He continued to write. "In exchange for the aforementioned sum, the party referred to as Dennis Fast, of 14 Highbury New Park, agrees to give up, surrender and allow the use of, without let or hindrance, a fixed quantity off the end of his life; the amount being mutually agreed at seven years."

"I should live so long!" said Mr Fishbane. "Why so generous, sonny?"

"For a million pounds, Mr Fishbane, I assure you that the Courts would expect something substantial."

"So seven years it is," sighed Mr Fishbane, blinking at the clerk's script that was so minute no human eye could have read it unaided. "Is it all in order now? I'm afraid my old eyes ain't strong enough to read your legal hand, sonny."

"It's all in order, Mr Fishbane. I promise you, there's not a judge on the Bench who'd laugh this one out."

The clerk smiled. His employer would have been proud of him. No human being could have wriggled out of the finely tangled mesh he'd drawn up. Not even a fly could have crept through it. Every eventuality had been covered; every loop-hole sealed. Even if Mr Fishbane had been the devil, the solicitor's clerk had tied him hand and foot.

The old man took the offered pen, and Mr Fast, aiming to humour him till the end, remarked jocularly, "I always understood such bargains as ours are signed in blood, Mr Fishbane, not ordinary ink."

"Very true, sonny," sighed Mr Fishbane. "But I ain't got so much to spare as I had in the old days. So if you'll excuse me, I'll sign in this beetroot soup. After all, it's the same colour."

The clerk nodded and grinned. The old man signed, then the clerk took the pen and added his own name in the watery red.

"Lawyers' deeds," he murmured, once again [...]ing his waggish employer. "Red in tooth and clause!"

Even though he dismissed the old fool's claims to unnatural eminence as crazy fancies, he was relieved that no flash of lightning or roll of thunder accompanied the signing of the Contract. The only disquieting thing was Mr Fast's accidentally knocking his decanter off the table. He picked it up and saw with annoyance that it was cracked. He turned it round and round. The crack was echoed in every facet; and the little clerks in their glittering cells stared out in sudden dismay. Slowly from the decanter's bowl, the dark wine dripped and leaked away . . .

He shrugged his shoulders and wished the old man good-night. Whether or not anything would come of the night's work remained to be seen. But Mr Fast, though of a cautious disposition, could not restrain a curious confidence that he had not wasted his time. He whistled as he mounted the area steps—and smirked as he thought of the old dolt painfully attempting to decipher the Contract's small print. His ancient face had looked so pathetically, almost tragically, baffled. One had to get up very early in the morning to get the better of Dennis Fast!

3 The morning was brilliant; the late October sun was affixed to the sky by a couple of tapes of pinkish cloud—like some large Agreement to Purchase. Mr Fast, on his way to Lamb's Court, looked up at it all and mentally wrote his dreams in the wide, blank spaces, filling them up with small print. His confidence in Mr Fishbane, though a little shaken in the light of day, had by no means gone.

It was true that, on wakening, he'd examined his rooms on the off-chance of the old man's having slipped something behind the cushions or under the carpet, but had found nothing but camphor balls, none of which had been miraculously changed into rubies or emeralds. Naturally he'd experienced a mild feeling of disappointment—however unreasonable in the circumstances; yet he was unable to suppress an inexplicable hope, and continued to give fate, circumstance or what you will every chance of fulfilling Mr Fishbane's strange Contract. He looked in gutters for stray glitterings; he took a cab for a short distance and felt behind the worn leather seats; and when he reached the office he sat at his desk in a state of continual expectation of interesting news.

His dreams were necessarily vague as he could not quite come to terms with the size of the old man's promise; but they had a brightness to them that lent his eyes an unusual shine. Memories of childhood desires and ambitions tended to play hide and seek in the secret passages of his mind, peeping out furtively in the shape of domed palaces by a dreaming sea, forests, proud horses and dogs with eyes like melted chocolate . . .

"Head in the clouds, Fast?" inquired his fellow clerk, who'd addressed him several times without response.

"Just valuing them for Probate," answered Mr Fast, very much in their employer's vein.

The morning wore on in all its serpentine detail. Clients came and went, and Mr Fast watched his bland employer smile them in and smile them out of the quiet, respectable room where all the recorded sin of the land, bound in calf, grazed on shelves from ceiling to floor.

When would his news come—and in what shape? Would the old gentleman call himself, or would he send a representative with powers of attorney? He toyed with this latter notion, observing each caller in meticulous detail to see if he fitted so momentous a role. But behind every pair of eyes, and in every pair of hands—fidgeting with hats, clutching long, coffin-like envelopes, or twisting gloves and handkerchiefs into unholy knots—the shrewd clerk saw only the habitual despair of customers of the law.

It was almost lunch-time before Mr Fast's hopes began to wither and fade. A cold thought had crept into his mind and cast a blight on it. There would be no news. There could be no caller from Mr Fishbane either on that morning or any other. The old man did not know the Lamb's Court address. The clerk had omitted to tell him.

A feeling of agitation and dismay came over him; he

cursed himself for the oversight. Lamb's Court, Mr Fishbane! he whispered inside his head. Morris and Morris of Lamb's Court, sir!

If only that uncanny power he'd had over the old man's mind during the previous evening would reach out once more! Lamb's Court! he repeated with the fiercest urgency. That's where your friend Dennis is!

"Mr Morris, please?"

A rosy-faced gentleman with black hair and a soft smile poked his head round the outer door.

"From Mr Fishbane?" breathed the clerk, irresistibly persuaded by the promptness of the visitation that his own will had achieved it.

"No," said the newcomer.

"Are you sure?" pursued the clerk, helplessly.

The newcomer gazed at him with a mixture of surprise and downright irritation, and Mr Fast was forced to remember what and where he was. He began hastily to apologise for his impertinence when his employer emerged from his room and greeted the stranger who turned out to be a respected colleague.

The solicitors retired and Mr Fast bit his lip in uneasy vexation. He really must control himself. The fantastic hopes engendered by Mr Fishbane were wreaking havoc with his peace of mind; his nightly dreams were invading his day.

"Mr Fast. Would you be so good as to step this way?"

Mr Morris had summoned him. Had the visitor complained of his rudeness? Mr Fast felt sick at heart. He entered the room and fixed his eyes on the patterned carpet.

"Sit down, Mr Fast."

Mr Morris was motioning him to the clients' chair. Confusedly, the clerk sat down—a thing he'd never done before in his employer's presence. The visitor, who had been standing by the fire, smiled and moved to stand beside him; Mr Morris, a fat and arrogant man in soft shoes, moved lightly to command the other side. The clerk felt overwhelmed by

an odour of barber's lotion that came at him in waves. It reminded him strongly of chrysanthemums. Mr Morris rubbed his hands together and seemed to bounce slightly.

"Since you have been with us, Mr Fast, how many wills would you say have passed through our hands?"

Bewildered, the clerk watched Mr Morris's oozing hands as if his employer was about to perform some legal conjuring trick and all the wills would come leaking out, one by one.

"A—a great many, sir."

"And how many legacies have, ha-ha! escaped us, Mr Fast?"

Mr Morris's fingers were twined in such intricately fluid knots that it seemed only the tiniest legacy might have slipped through unsqueezed.

"Many hundreds, sir."

"Yes indeed. We are always the bridesmaid, never the blushing bride!" Here he opened his hands in a gesture at once benevolent and resigned. "But now, my dear Mr Fast, your turn has come. A bouquet was thrown—and you caught it. After all these years, my friend, you too are a beneficiary! Allow me to congratulate you! A beneficiary, Mr Fast. A Bride of Probate!"

"Fishbane!" gasped the clerk unbelievingly. "It's Fishbane!"

"There he goes again!" chuckled the visitor whose name was Johns. " Was his father in kippers, Morris, eh, eh?"

"Your father, Mr Fast—"

"Dead, sir; dead these twenty-five years!"

"I know that sir. How else could you benefit? Come, come! Where is your law? Your father, it turns out, owned a bit of property."

"Near Kimberley," put in Mr Johns.

"Which is in Africa," explained Mr Morris.

"And I represent certain business interests," said Mr Johns, "who wish to purchase it."

"Diamonds," murmured Mr Morris, leaning down to

within inches of the clerk's ear, "have been found."

"A figure has been mentioned," breathed Mr Johns, taking charge of the other ear.

"But not yet agreed."

"However, Mr Morris and I—"

"Feel it our duty to advise you."

"Close with the offer, sir."

"A very considerable sum indeed—"

The two solicitors' voices seemed to be meeting at some Speakers' Corner inside his head, and in a strong wind. Words buffeted against each other; the inner air was filled with them.

The heat in the room grew oppressive; his eyes misted so that the multitudinous books seemed to be writhing against each other like fatted maggots about to rupture and disgorge their unwholesome contents: dreary battalions of secret wretches whose muddled crimes and iron punishments had built the ramparts of the law. The shelves were crawling with them. They jostled on the mahogany precipices with arms outstretched—then tumbled down into a monstrous black wastepaper basket that resembled Mr Fishbane's cemetery silk hat.

"Why, you look as pale as a client, Mr Fast," rumbled Mr Morris. "It must be the chair!"

But Mr Johns, being less fanciful, was of the opinion it was shock, and that the young man had not rightly taken in his good fortune.

"Don't you understand, sir, that your father struck it lucky, as they say—albeit, posthumously. A remarkably shrewd man, your father."

Dazedly Mr Fast attempted to remember his father; a feckless businessman whose affairs had had more ups and downs than a drunkard's elbow. Though the ups had never been much to boast of, the downs had been simply tremendous. It had been on a down that he'd perished, and his wife, like Jill in the rhyme, had followed soon after. Their Effects had been done up in brown paper and their seven year old

son had been bequeathed to an orphanage in the Penton-
ville Road. Now Mr Fast was asked to believe that that
brown paper had contained a Deed to diamonds. He could
not believe it.

"Fishbane," he whispered. "It must be Fishbane."

"Is that, ha-ha! what your father died of?" asked Mr
Morris with a sympathetic smirk.

"A figure has been mentioned," insisted Mr Johns.

"Only fair to tell you," recollected Mr Morris.

"Very considerable sum—"

"In the region of one million pounds—"

"Fishbane!" cried the clerk. "For God's sake, admit it's
from Fishbane!" He clutched at Mr Johns's coat. It was horribly important to him to know that Mr Fishbane was an
ordinary old man who had worked this wonder by ordinary
means. Abjectly he stared from solicitor to solicitor for some
veiling of their eyes, for some shrug of evasion that would
tell him they knew more than they said.

"My dear young man," said Mr Johns, disengaging himself. "I assure you we know absolutely nothing of anyone
or anything called Fishbane. If you fancy there is a mysterious benefactor, you are quite mistaken. All is entirely above
board. Your good fortune comes to you from your dead
father. Be grateful, sir. Accept it as the miracle it is."

"The miracle it is," repeated the clerk; and felt for a moment that his chair was poised in the middle of a nothingness
that stretched to the end of time. The fear that had been
gnawing at the dark of his mind since the previous evening
had at last sprung out to glare him in the eye. *Who was the
old man in the basement?*

A cab was called to take Mr Fast back to Highbury New
Park. Smiles, congratulations and handshakes were heaped
on him like bouquets; and it was only when the cab door
snapped shut and he was encased in the black leather casket
that his thoughts began to stir.

The old man in the basement. The very expression had a most suggestive ring to it. He shook his head. The idea—which he positively refused to put into words—was too nightmarish to be taken seriously. After all, the million pounds hadn't arrived with a reek of sulphur. Two solicitors had been concerned; and that was as far removed from fancy, hellish or otherwise, as mortal man could get.

He glanced out of the window as the cab rattled northward through the City streets, and the everyday sights restored him to a more reasonable view of his situation. His good fortune following so closely on his mysterious conversation and signing of the Contract had been no more than an extraordinary coincidence. Long experience of the law had taught him that stranger things had happened.

He nodded; but was unable to rid himself altogether of an uneasy feeling that if he hadn't signed the Contract he would not now be a millionaire. In view of this uneasiness—which tended to increase as the cab jolted nearer and nearer to Highbury New Park—he couldn't help feeling relieved that he'd taken the old man sufficiently seriously to be careful about the drawing up of the Contract.

He ventured a little dry chuckle in his leathery seclusion as he recalled his own ingenuity. The small print, Mr Fishbane—whoever you may be! Have you read the small print yet, sir? You may have your insurance, Mr Fishbane; but I also have mine!

A feeling of tremendous contentment came over him and he settled back to contemplate the possession of a million pounds. He attempted to summon up the morning's dreams —but his mind was still in a whirlwind. He could only catch at fragments on the outskirts of his thoughts; strange, almost grotesque confusions of forests growing inside mansions, horses with the heads of dogs, and gleaming railway engines that rushed soundlessly over glass-cool seas.

At last he gave up and reflected that immense wealth must be like new boots that needed to be worn in before giving comfort. Tomorrow, after a good night's sleep, perhaps, his thoughts would be more ordered. All his dreams would come back to him and he would be able to sit in his chair as before a banquet—and eat of it to his heart's content.

But I must tell the old man, he chuckled to himself as the cab turned into Highbury New Park, and see how he takes the news. His bleary old eyes will pop out of his head and his wits will be turned tighter than a corkscrew. He's sure to fancy his nonsense had something to do with it! I must be absolutely sure to tell him before he has a chance to hear it from someone else, otherwise there's no telling what he'll claim.

The cab halted; the clerk was home. He got out and paid the driver and sauntered to the area railings. Sharp as a crow in his tattered black, Mr Fishbane was standing below. He squinted up at Mr Fast.

"A million pounds, eh, sonny? I told you I could afford it."

A feeling of extreme terror seized the clerk. He glared down at the old man. All thoughts but the Contract had gone from his head. What had he done? Then he remembered his cunning insurance.

"The small print, Mr Fishbane! Have you read the small print?"

The old man's face seemed to shrink a little. He shook his head as if in despair. Then he stretched out his arm in a gesture of pointing. Mr Fast looked. For an instant he fancied a faint shadow beside the old man. Hurriedly he looked away. He retreated from the area railings; his face was white, his heart was as cold as death.

4 Three good burying grounds served the district: the graveyard of the church for parishioners, a cemetery for Jews, and a well laid out, spacious plot where the only qualification for interment was that of being dead. In this latter place lay Dr Herz, in a sepulchre that resembled a marble drawer unaccountably full of gravel. The trembling clerk stood before it and glared at the inscription. "Taken suddenly, in the midst of his labours . . ."

"What were your labours, Dr Herz? Was it you who called *him* up and left him for me to find? Tell me—for pity's sake tell me, *is* he the devil?"

A passer-by stared with curiosity and pity at the shaken young man who muttered over a grave. Mr Fast reddened and smiled feebly. He was going out of his mind. That was it; Mr Johns had been quite right. Shock had unhinged him.

If matters didn't improve, he would go to a doctor. After all, he could afford the best. You understand, doctor, I keep thinking the devil lives downstairs. Ha-ha!

Or a priest. Why not have a word with some ninny of a curate or other? He'd be glad of the work. Might even make a name for himself. Come to think of it, what was wrong with a bishop, or a cardinal, or one of those dome-headed rabbis? Nothing like going right to the top when you could afford it. You see, Your Holiness, I signed this Contract with someone I have reason to believe was the devil . . .

It would really be no different from briefing counsel. The clerk couldn't help smiling at his bizarre thoughts; then he began to chuckle, and then to laugh. He laughed till the tears ran down his face and old Dr Herz's grave jumped and danced in their shimmering.

"Fishbane, you old imposter!" he gasped. "Trying to rob me of all joy in my father's million!"

"Rob you, sonny? I gave it to you."

Mr Fast cried out in alarm. The old man had been standing behind him. He stared at the tattered old scoundrel, and his terror gave way to a frantic anger. "And what if you did?" he muttered. "It was in the Contract. Haven't you read it right through? Haven't you read the small print yet?"

Once more the old man seemed to shrink away in dismay —and once more he pointed. The shadow was beside him again, and this time the clerk saw it had become a little more distinct. He caught his breath—and fled.

He rushed headlong from the cemetery and into Green Lanes, where a long row of villas, stretching, it seemed, to eternity—though in fact only to Manor House—stared him stonily in the face as if to bring him to his senses with their weight of bricks and mortar.

Who are you running from, Dennis Fast?

The old man and—

—And what?

Nothing—nothing! A trick of light and shade.

Then go back.

No!

Why not? Was it really only a trick of shade and light? What else?

A trick of yours, perhaps. A trick in the Contract, in the small print?

He returned to his apartment and sank into his tomb of a chair where presently he drifted into a dark sleep, empty of dreams. Next morning he awoke with a dull pain in his head; but the grotesque panic that had remained with him until he'd drifted off had disappeared. His mood was one of sombre anger and resolution to crush his appalling thoughts and fancies. He changed his sleep-crumpled clothes, discarding each garment like an outgrown fear. There is no devil, there is no hell; there is only an old man in the basement, stinking of beetroot soup. Highbury New Park, Lamb's Court and my million pounds are real. Everything else is but a dream's child.

For a moment, the panic returned. He had meant to say, a child's dream; but his thoughts seemed to tangle of their own accord. Carefully, but with shaking hands, he encased himself in his best suit and left the house, casting only a cursory glance through the area railings. The basement was quiet. The clerk walked away. It no longer seemed to matter very much who and what the old man was. The day was bright, the world was wide, and Mr Fast was a millionaire.

He walked in the direction of the City, stopping every now and again to stare fixedly in shop windows, then turning away with a dull sneer. Everything was thin and tawdry; there was nothing he saw that would hold its value but in the child of an eye.

He bit his lip. The *eye* of a *child*! What was wrong with him? He hurried on, pushing his way through the increasing crowds. The shops no longer attracted him. What was the point of spending what he'd sold his soul to obtain?

But he hadn't sold it; or at least, not in the generally accepted sense. The bargain he'd struck had been a very different kettle of fish—as any close reader of small print would have seen directly.

"Out of my way!" he muttered, as someone made to cross in front of him.

"It's not me who's in your way, sonny."

The abominable Mr Fishbane turned and squinted at him.

"Pig!" snarled the clerk. "Crazy, lying pig! Leave me alone! Go get yourself some spectacles and read the Contract! *Then* see what your rights are! Or have you read it already?"

The old man stared silently into the clerk's distorted face. The clerk shrank back against a wall. He averted his eyes, but not before the old man had pointed to his side. The shadow. Day by day, hour by hour, it was growing more and more distinct.

What was this shade that had come out of the clean sunlight to linger beside the terrible old man? If the clerk knew, he dared not confess it, even to himself. In the deepest part of his mind he denied it, struggled to blot it out; dared not even pronounce its name for fear of giving it substance more rapidly than its present remorseless growth. It was a queer battle that he waged—a battle to escape from a Contract that had been woven with such dexterity that not even a fly could have crept through its fine drawn mesh.

Dimly he sensed that his chief hope lay in his dreams. Only in them could he escape and enjoy his miraculous wealth. By day and night he struggled to clutch at them; but his brain was too slow. His thoughts seemed to be congealing inside his head and he felt an aching thickness in which all longing was being crushed. Perhaps he had caught some foul disease that was going to cut him off before he could so much as broach his fortune? No . . . no; it was not that.

He continued to meet with Mr Fishbane—sometimes in Green Lanes, sometimes in the City when Mr Fast called at Lamb's Court to verify the fact of his inheritance, and sometimes in the cemetery where Dr Herz was buried. And always the old man squinted at him as if surprised and distressed by his pallor and air of deathly strain.

"The riches of the world, sonny. What has become of

them?"

For answer, Mr Fast would stare at him and whisper, "The Contract. What has become of the Contract?", and then tremble as the shadow crept out from under the old man's tattered wing of an arm, and lingered unmistakeably in his sight.

With extraordinary desperation and urgency he tried to force himself to dream again. He sensed that the battle he'd been engaged in had changed into a pursuit and that very little time remained before he would be caught. So powerfully did he try that he did indeed succeed in dreaming, but not as he would have wished.

He dreamed of gracious mansions that, as soon as he signed the title deeds and possessed them, shuddered and turned to rat-infested corruption. He dreamed of lovely women and laughing children clustering about·him, clinging to his coat tails. Eagerly he looked into their faces. Their eyes shone; merciful heaven! they were golden sovereigns! Pair by pair he plucked them out and clinked them into a black leather bag. Now the sightless beauties blundered about in a void until at last they vanished, leaving him in an iron solitude that grew darker and darker until he awoke.

This curious dream occurred at the beginning of November on a Friday night, when the smell of beetroot soup had been suffocatingly strong so that the sense of entombment when the clerk awoke seemed as much a consequence of the old man's cooking as anything more terrible.

The morning turned out to be brilliant and precise; though, like all precision, there was more light in it than warmth, for a wintry chill seemed to have reached forward.

Leadenly, the clerk dressed himself. He must go out; perhaps there'd be some remedy for his sickly condition in sunlight.

Mr Fishbane was standing in the area. He appeared to have been sunning himself; there was a faint pinkish tinge in his withered cheeks.

"A fine day, sonny."

The words boomed and clanged in the clerk's head as if

the arched bone had been changed into a great bell. "Day—
ay—ay—ay—"

"Why do you torment me?"

"Me? I don't torment anybody, my dear. Believe me—
ye—ye—ye—"

"Liar! Swindler!"

"Is it the Contract you mean? The very small print, eh?"
He fumbled in his coat. "You see, sonny, I've taken your
advice. I've gone out and bought myself a pair of spectacles.
I've read the small print—"

The clerk's heart turned to stone.

"Crafty, weren't you, Mr Fast? Cartloads of monkeys,
eh? Well—well, I blame myself. I should have been more
cautious."

He twisted the spectacles so that the lenses caught the light
and a pair of suns blazed pitilessly in the clerk's eyes.

"You've turned me into a robber, sonny; and believe me,
I never meant it. But—but one can't help taking one's hat
off to you!" Here he chuckled, but there was no merriment
in it. "Seven years off the end of your life! But *which end*,
eh? How could I have guessed that you'd take such a sly
advantage and slip in the *first* end, so to speak? I never
dreamed that you'd sell me your childhood, Mr Fast!"

The old man put on his new spectacles and raised his
sheltering arm. Beside him stood the shade that was no
longer a shade. It was clear and distinct in every damning
detail. The vagueness that had been in its steady building out
of nothingness was all dispersed. On the previous occasion
there had been only black holes at the ends of its sleeves; now
pale young fingers had grown in every particular. They
twisted and fluttered towards Mr Fishbane's mittened hand.

The old man moved aside so as not to impede the clerk's
view. The phantom stood in the merciless sunshine: a little
boy of seven, dressed in an old-fashioned sailor's suit. Its
hair was fair and curling; its face was of an unearthly pallor.
The clerk gave a harsh scream and clutched onto the area
railings. He glared down in rage and terror at the ghost of
his own childhood.

part two

1 Down the endless streets, avenues, roads, lanes and crescents whose names were epitaphs to a green life long buried under the grey—Mountgrove, Woodberry, Seven Sisters, Brownswood—trudged the clerk who'd sold his childhood to the old man in the basement. His terror had now subsided into a gnawing anger that seemed to embrace the world.

The old man had swindled him. Left behind in the property he'd sold, had been certain items not specified in the Contract. The old man had no right to them; no Court of Law would uphold his claim. Neither in the large nor the small print had there been any mention of them; the old man was an embezzler and a thief.

Locked securely in the childhood the rich clerk had disposed of had been his dreams, yearnings and the very springs of his desire. Now they were gone. Little by little he'd felt them slip away until all was empty within. This was the sickness that oppressed him: the grey gloom, the listless despair and the feeble hatred for everything that moved or shone. Passion, longing, remembrance and even love itself had withered with horrible rapidity—for their roots had been cut. The soul—or, rather, the half soul— he'd so cunningly preserved was now entombed within him, as still and cold as death.

A dull panic rose up inside him; but not even this hateful sensation could survive in the chill of his iron head. Only the Law remained, unmoved by hell and disaster, the loss of dreams and the severing of souls.

Even as the thought occurred, the thin, bent figure of the clerk seemed to straighten—and the sun, precise as ever, took an inventory of the change in his shadow which lifted abruptly off the pavement and now limped from iron railing to iron railing like a cripple with a twisted crutch.

The railings gave way to a park gate and the clerk, his head groaning with writs and executions and the distress of chattels such as a child's hopes, found himself walking across a patch of tattered grass. As he stared down he was reminded of the frayed green carpet in counsel's Chambers where, on legal business, he had sometimes gone as if to church.

Indeed, the Chambers were the holiest place he knew; in them the most intimate affairs of mankind were weighed and measured in a voice that flowed like holy oil. Counsel's opinion . . . counsel's opinion . . .

A Writ of *distringas*, Mr Fast? The word entered his head like a snake.

The plaintiff shall have a *distringas* to compel the defendant to deliver the goods, obligingly explained the voice in his head, in case he'd forgotten, and the sheriff shall summon an inquest to determine the value of the goods.

I know, I know, answered the clerk impatiently; and then added more politely: beyond calculation, sir, I do assure you.

Come, come, Mr Fast! went on this other voice, continuing the inward conversation. Nothing is beyond calculation. Everything must and shall be reduced to terms of money. There is no other way. What was the amount this Mr Fishbane paid you?

A million pounds—

Generous, Mr Fast. It would seem to the Court that any loss you have sustained has been amply compensated. After all, Mr Fast—look at it reasonably. You have disposed of— shall we say—a second-hand childhood; and now it turns out that certain childishly interesting items were left behind in the pockets, so to speak. But it is not really to be compared with a second-hand suit that still has some wear in it. No one can re-live a used childhood. In the opinion of Counsel, Mr Fast, it would appear you've done remarkably well for yourself and have shown an unusual astuteness throughout. Your injuries are trifling—amounting perhaps to a few pence only—and your profit has been enormous. Rejoice, Mr Fast. Rejoice!

The clerk looked up. The grass had sloped down to a pretty pond laced about with iron hoops. At the water's edge, half a dozen pigeons and a family of ducks were fiercely contending for crumbs. An old man and a little boy were feeding them; an old man in shabby black who re- sembled an ancient bird himself—and a little boy in a sailor's suit.

The clerk cried out in dread.

Pooh! Mr Fast—a child! Not even that. An insubstantial ghost—an apparition—a phantom such as could not even take the oath! You are a rich man, Mr Fast; it is Counsel's opinion that you should not sweat and shudder at ghosts in the bright sun.

But despite advice, the clerk did sweat and shudder; for a ghost in the sunshine is a fearful thing.

I beg you, consider your great wealth. I wish it were mine. I really do. I would know what to do with it.

What?

Ah—well. I'd need notice of that question. But if I were in your shoes I fancy I'd attempt to purchase back the items unluckily included in the sale. Would not a reasonable offer be acceptable to the parties concerned? Put yourself in the child's place, Mr Fast. Counsel advises you to get the old man out of the way—and deal with the phantom child. A shrewd fellow like you should be able to swindle it out of every dream in its bloodless little head.

Mr Fishbane bent and nudged the child who turned, squinting shyly in the sun. It encountered the clerk's bleak and dreadful gaze; it shrank away, seeking refuge in the black folds of the old man's coat.

Get rid of Mr Fishbane, urged the counsel inside Mr Fast's head.

Mr Fishbane cast the last of his crumbs and dusted himself down.

"Do me a favour, Mr Fast," he said abruptly, giving the clerk a shadowy smile. "Look after this little boy for me while I pay a call in the neighbourhood."

He disengaged himself from the child. "Dennis, my love; Mr Fast will walk with you in the sun. You know Mr Fast, don't you? He lives upstairs. He'll be kind to you. Trust me, Dennis . . ."

Before the clerk could answer, Mr Fishbane had flapped and shuffled away at a surprisingly rapid pace—as if some other Contract was on the brink of exchange.

He still obeys your thoughts. You hardly know your own strength, Mr Fast. You are a very remarkable fellow. Now —pluck the child!

Eerily and with faltering step the clerk approached the little boy. He held out his hand—and the child took it. The clerk stifled a cry of horror and disgust. The sensation had been extraordinary. Though the child's hand nested entirely within his palm, he felt cold damp fingers engulf his whole hand.

Come, Mr Fast—we must do better than that. We must be natural and talk. We wouldn't want anyone to think the cat had got our tongue!

He began to walk—and the weird child drifted along beside him. He longed to study it closely; but such glances as he gave were met with so piercing a look of accusation that he could not sustain it.

Talk—talk, Mr Fast! Take advantage, sir!

"He—Mr Fishbane—called you Dennis. Is that your name?"

The phantom nodded.

Good—good! Put the witness at his ease. Lead him gently to the slaughter!

"Do you know I am a rich man, Dennis? Would you like me to buy you something?"

Oh excellent, Mr Fast! A real stroke, that!

A smile flickered across the child's face; but the clerk had an uncanny feeling that it was in response to some inner voice that remained quite secret.

The park had become more formal in aspect. Flower beds inhabited by pale waxen autumn blooms lay on either side of the path; and the air was scented with the smell of burning leaves. The white-faced clerk and the death-faced child in the old-fashioned sailor's suit walked hand in hand. Passers by were intrigued by the curious sight. The clerk felt embarrassed. Continual glances, half smiling, half wistful, disturbed him. An elderly couple approached. They were plainly well-to-do; the clerk moved to let them by. But they paused, and the lady gazed at Mr Fast's childhood—all curls and fragile pallor in its quaint sailor's suit.

"Charming," she murmured. "Quite charming."

The clerk started; and then felt absurdly flattered. He raised his hat and hoped the lady could see the resemblance. So far as he could remember, it was the first time anyone had called him charming. He felt strangely proud of the little boy . . .

"And will he be a sailor when he grows up?" she asked laughingly.

"An admiral, I'm sure," said her husband, whose weathered face strongly suggested he'd been in the same line himself.

Mr Fast looked down at the phantom child. "Answer the lady, Dennis. Has the cat got your tongue? Come—tell the lady what you dream of being."

"An engine driver," whispered the little ghost—to the clerk's humiliation and defeated rage.

"Not an admiral, all in gold braid?" pursued the gentleman, reminiscently.

"An engine driver," repeated the eerie child, and its voice was like the rustling of leaves.

"Liar!" hissed the clerk when the couple had gone. "Little liar! You must know very well what you'll be! A solicitor's clerk. Why did you lie? Are you ashamed of me? What about my million, eh? Had you forgotten?"

"A million?" whispered the child; and its eyes gleamed secretly. Ghost though it was, composed of vapours, dreams and the severed half of a soul, it was yet a child. It turned its bloodless little face towards the clerk as if dreading that the rich man's offer to buy it something had been forfeited by its lie about its dream.

"Come!" breathed the clerk, his hopes renewed. "I'll buy you whatever your heart desires. Anything—anything in the world. What are your dreams, sonny? Just tell Mr Fast—and Mr Fast will see what he can do."

Oh very cunning, Mr Fast. One has to take off one's wig to you!

Beyond the park on its further side lay a curious muddle of shops and street markets—once a village but long since engulfed in the grey fist of the town. Pavements overflowed with every human want and need: buckets, bowls, sauce-pans, pyramids of china cups resembling domed eastern cities proudly built on hills, perambulators, garden cherubs and a witches' stable of brooms that were being forever tumbled down by urchins and ancient ladies past the age of flying.

Shouts and cries made a fine music in the air as the riches of the world changed hands at bargain prices.

"Silver salt cellar, mister. B'longed to the mad Tsar of Russia so them dents is historic!" A trader, whose face had as many dents as his wares and was possibly even more historic, plucked at the clerk and the pale, bloodless child in a sailor's suit. "Two shillin's and you're robbing me!"

The child's lips parted at the bright piece of silver cracked and scored by the legendary rages of a mad king.

"Buy the little 'un a pocket knife, mister—the very thing for a sailor!" A horny hand held out an object like an iron spider. "Blades fer Indies' fruits, pens, cleaning yer nails, lifting tar out of 'orses' 'ooves and powder out of cannons, scissors and cigar-cutters! Mother-of-pearl and silver. Property of Lord Nelson!"

But the clerk pushed by with savage contempt—and the phantom child drifted after, its weird eyes gleaming wistfully for Nelson's miraculous knife.

"'air brushes fer yore nipper's golden curls, mister. Genuine tortoise-shell; come off the Queen of Sheba's tortoise! God strike me dead if I tell a lie!"

At last they reached the limits of this village that had been entombed alive; they turned into an alley of uncanny quiet where the shadows of the tall houses lay along the road like strips of undertaker's crêpe. The air smelled of glue and sawn wood.

"Look, sonny—look at that!"

The clerk halted. One of the houses was got up as a shop. It had been a cabinet-maker's but had turned itself into a kind of toyshop. The owner, long since retired from life size, had gone into the miniature where a good craftsman can play God. He made dolls' houses and the tiny furniture to go in them. In the window was his latest and most ambitious creation. A marvellous model of St Paul's Cathedral, complete with tiny congregation and minute, gold-plated bells that would toll to the touch of ropes as fine as hair. Down the wide steps tripped a little family, precise in pinpoint silks and rich mouse furs, to their carriage that waited eternally by the statue of good Queen Anne. A perfect long ago Sunday that would never change. And, as a mischievous quirk of humour, the cabinet-maker had left his spectacles in little Ludgate Hill, quite blocking it and attracting half a dozen thumb high passers by who stood and stared in consternation at so gigantic a construction in gold and glass.

"Do you want it?" asked the clerk, fascinated by the topsyturvydom a single stroke had made. But the phantom child shook its head. Its eyes were huge and lost-looking, as if the cabinet-maker's little joke had destroyed a world of dreams. But to the clerk, the very destruction of the tiny dream had been its joy. It had seemed like an ingenious Writ or Injunction served on the lawless soul. He turned on the child in uncomprehending bitterness.

"What *is* it you want, then?"

But the phantom was no longer at his side. He saw it at the end of the alleyway; the sunlight flashed on the brass buttons of its suit—and it vanished.

"Come back!" he cried out in dismay. The child had given him no chance. He must catch it before it was reclaimed by the implacable Mr Fishbane! He rushed in pursuit, and indeed caught a glimpse of its pallid face and frantic fingers twisting and darting among the market crowds.

He pushed and elbowed his way on with panic-stricken urgency; but the shoppers and traders and damnable urchins who scuttled among them like villainous mice, clogged his steps and swallowed up the wraith he pursued. Even when he broke free he could still feel their breath in his face and the sharp buffeting as they retaliated with boot, fist and umbrella. He swayed, staggered—closed his eyes for a moment . . . Ah! there it was at last! Playing in the gutter with a crazy bit of twisted iron. He rushed forward and clutched at the child.

A thin face, sharp as a splinter, glared up at him in fury and surprise.

"Wotcher want, mister?"

The clerk stared down at a fair-haired urchin in tattered blue.

"What's 'e want?"

A little girl, as foul and ragged as the boy, appeared from the crowded nowhere.

"Bleedin' busybody. Finks 'e's a copper. Get yer own 'oop, mister." Threateningly the urchin in blue raised the twisted iron, which, in spite of efforts to bang it into a circle, still strongly resembled one of the railings about the pond in the park. Suddenly the little girl gave the clerk a push. Fury seized him; he made to kick the little thief—but the urchin was ready. Long experience had taught him what to expect. The clerk's elastic-sided boot was neatly trapped in the stolen railing. As he toppled and fell, he heard a voice screech in his ear: "I 'opes to see yer frizzlin' in 'ell, mister— like an 'aporth of sausage!"

He climbed to his feet and hastened away; his limbs were bruised and trembling. He had lost the phantom with all his possessions still in its heart. Counsel's opinion had failed him; and that was a frightful thing.

The gleaming shops and arcades mocked him as he passed them by; he was utterly obsessed with the notion that he could do nothing until he had placated the ghost he had sold into damnation.

Then he saw the hoop. It was in an arcade, hanging high among kites, paper lanterns and grinning puppets which dangled as though they'd been executed by order of some infant Judge. A magnificent hoop, painted silver and with coloured glass buttons glued round the rim. An eternity ring for a lady giant; and there was a silver stick to bang it along. Remembering the urchin in the gutter with his awkward theft, the clerk knew that no child, living or dead, could have resisted this hoop. He was amazed by how cheap it was. Thirty shillings. Good heavens! it must have been worth ten times as much! Eagerly he made the purchase and hurried back towards Highbury New Park, craftily delighted at having obtained so rich a bargain. Already he felt quite redeemed . . .

Suddenly there was a violent commotion in the air and a sound of iron thunder. A black shadow engulfed him and down streamed a shower of fire. He all but shrieked aloud in terror—when he saw he'd walked under the railway bridge that crossed Seven Sisters' Road, and a train had passed overhead, scattering tiny cinders as it went. He mopped his brow and dusted his ash-dappled hat.

Calm yourself, Mr Fast. Did you fancy you'd been snatched into hell—right out of the middle of Seven Sisters' Road? No one goes to hell anymore, Mr Fast. Take Counsel's opinion on it. Besides, it would hardly be *you* who'd go, sir.

At last he reached Number Fourteen Highbury New Park. The basement was full of shadows. He peered through the iron railings. No one was there; it looked as if it had been empty for days. He went down and banged and kicked on the door. Then he returned to his own apartment; his face was grey with a youthless age. He was too late; the ghost of his childhood, with all his longings, hopes and dreams, had gone with the terrible old man.

2 The house was uncannily quiet. The clerk walked
from room to room with no sound but the oc-
casional crackling of camphor balls as he trod on
the carpet's edge. Where had the old man and the
phantom child gone? What became of half souls
sold into damnation? Were there really flames? For a moment he fancied a smell of burning skin in his nostrils. He
shuddered and drew the curtains, as if to shut out the gathering gloom. He had the strangest idea that the darkness was
all rising up from the basement like some black, airless tide.
He lit the gas mantles—all of them—and went to the side-

board. The cracked decanter was empty; the dregs of the port had dried in a rusty, brownish ring. He stared at it for some minutes, seeing nothing—not even his own reflection; then his eye was caught by the glittering silver hoop he'd propped against the wall. A harsh sob escaped him; but whether it was of pain, anger or despair, there was no telling. It had come quite unbidden—as did the tears that suddenly flooded his eyes.

There was a noise in the street outside. Mr Fast sat up in bed and listened. At first he supposed it to be part of a dream and therefore in his head; but it was certainly outside. It was a regular clanging and rolling sound. It grew steadily louder, then stopped and began again, dwindling this time until it was almost gone. But not quite. The moment's silence was repeated, then back came the rolling and banging, passing directly under his window.

He got up and went to open the front door. The street lay in cold, still moonlight, its every detail as sharp as bone. Doors, windows, steps and railings were as precise as the cabinet-maker's marvellous toy; and along the pavement ran a little boy in a sailor's suit, banging a makeshift iron hoop. His bleached, almost transparent face wore an intent expression as he kept the hoop rolling with his stick.

"Dennis!" breathed the clerk. The phantom glanced at him, but did not stop till it reached the end of the road when it turned and began again. Filled with a wild hope, the clerk rushed back to his apartment and snatched up the silver hoop. Eagerly he returned and stumbled down the steps into the cold street. It was long past midnight and all Highbury New Park was safely abed; the fantastic clerk in his nightgown was as private as a dream.

"Dennis!" he whispered—and the little ghost in its sailor's suit came running and tapping towards him. "Here! A new hoop. Look how it shines in the moonlight! A real treasure. Thirty silver shillings it cost. It's yours! Take it!"

He held it out; but the phantom's intentness did not falter. It was utterly absorbed in the control of its bent and battered toy—touching it now this side, now that, as if it were a living thing. The little ghost flickered past the clerk and his glittering gift as if they didn't exist. Pleadingly he called after it:

"Please take it! Take it and tell me what is in your heart!"

He began to run, clumsily; when the phantom turned and came dancing back on the freezing moonlight. Tap . . . tap . . . tap went the stick on the hoop, and on the apparition's face there seemed to be a smile of deep delight.

"For pity's sake, don't leave me! Don't you see, we are one? There's but one heart and soul between us! There must be no secrets. We are rich, my Dennis—so rich! All the treasures of the world are ours! Only, only you *must* tell me what it is we want. Dennis—Dennis!"

The phantom's teeth gleamed in the moonlight as its cold lips parted in silent laughter; once more it passed the clerk by. Despairingly now he pursued it, his nightgown fluttering awkwardly about his ankles and threatening to bring him down. And as he ran, he banged the silver hoop along with the silver stick till he and his phantom childhood were almost side by side in the moon grey street.

But Mr Fast had lost his old skill. While the ghost was deft, he stumbled so that the extravagant hoop wobbled madly and clattered against area railings. He struggled to recapture the lost cunning, panting:

"It will come back to me! Only wait . . . it will all come back! You'll see!"

For a short distance the painted hoop with its flashing glass jewels did indeed rattle on in fine style, even outdistancing the grotesque figure of the clerk in his nightgown. As it did so, an absurd pride filled Mr Fast; and the phantom's eyes grew dreamy . . .

"We'll buy a house, you and I. A great mansion somewhere, my Dennis. I know there was somewhere we always longed for. Oh my heart aches to know it again! Don't you feel the self-same pain? Tell me—and it will be ours.

Where, where was it, child?"

"In a tree," whispered the ghost, its eyes suddenly as sharp as a squirrel's. "In the great old oak at Hatfield? You remember? You were there!"

Then it seemed to chuckle in weird delight; it gazed at the clerk it was to become most knowingly.

"No!" groaned the clerk in baffled rage and misery. "There was more, I know! There were treasures, dreams, grand longings! You have them—you and the old man! Give them up! Don't you understand? They are mine! I swear I never sold them! What else was there? Tell me, what other dreams?"

"To be an engine driver," whispered the ghost. "An engine driver . . ."

The silver hoop, rolling on ahead, tipped and tilted and danced drunkenly into the gutter. With a cry of dismay the clerk sped forward to save it. He knelt to pick it up; then, still kneeling, he turned to face the oncoming spectre. Painfully he stretched out his arms as if to embrace it.

It seemed to drift into the very substance of his breast— and its iron hoop rolled grimly by. Cold, damp arms enfolded the clerk; and a black weight forced him backwards. The child's deathly face was close to his own. Its eyes were vague and secret; its lips were parted in its strange smile. He struggled to kiss the smooth white cheek—as if making some gesture of love and recognition. A stone answered his mouth.

A terrible fear swept through him, like a bitter wind; then anger followed—the old, hopeless anger that engulfed everything that quickened beyond his shrunken grasp. He reached up and seized the child's throat. He squeezed and squeezed till the strength went out of his fingers and the breath went out of his body. Then he let go; his face was dark and congested.

"Come back . . . forgive me . . ." he tried to cry out; but could utter no more than a harsh croaking. Even as he'd fought to strangle the child, fingers had tightened round his own throat, squeezing and squeezing with a wild and dreadful strength.

He staggered to gather up the fallen silver hoop; then he looked up and down the road. The phantom had gone. He saw something shining in the gutter. He fancied it was a sovereign. He picked it up and saw it was the brass button off a child's sailor suit. Savagely he flung it from him. Then he climbed the steps of Number Fourteen and went back into his sombre apartment. His shoulders were bent and shaking with helpless sobs; and in the moonlight the bruising of his neck showed up like the shadow of a rope.

3 The next night he heard the hoop again. He lay in bed, sweating profusely, but did not dare to go outside. On the following night also he heard it, beginning shortly after midnight and continuing for an hour or more.

During the day, however, he saw nothing of the old man and the little boy. Though he scoured the neighbouring streets and open places, he never so much as glimpsed them. Yet he knew they were still about. Very early in the mornings he heard sounds, and the stink of beetroot soup kept drifting up and sickening him; but when he went outside the basement always appeared to be deserted—as if it hadn't been lived in for years.

Hateful and frightening as were the eerie pair, their total disappearance during the day gnawed at the clerk with a newer terror. The very secrecy of it increased his sense of loneliness and enormous loss; and he brooded painfully on where Mr Fishbane might be leading the phantom child. What streets was it drifting down, what houses was it peering in; what fields, what lakes, what parks; was it even by the sea?

Did people stop and stare in the street at its neat, appealing pallor? Did they ask it what it would become? Was it perhaps at Hatfield, flickering round the great oaks; played with by children who, not knowing its horrible circumstance, took it for one of themselves?

These and other questions so tormented the clerk that he could think of nothing else; all his instincts were kept at the highest pitch to detect the smallest indication that would betray the strange pair's journeying out into their secret day.

He would lie with his ear pressed to the floor until a strong quiet fell when he would hasten outside as quickly as he could—only to discover the road to be empty and the basement as silent as the grave.

At last it occurred to him that he was being deliberately deceived and that they were still in the basement and only went out after he himself had gone. Accordingly he began his vigil on the living room floor, just under the window, with a plate of bread and cheese beside him, to sustain him through a longer stretch of the day.

As was usual, the faint sounds from downstairs continued for a short while and then an absolute silence fell. The clerk waited, scarcely daring to move. He observed the passage of time by the changing of shadows in the room and on the frontage of the houses opposite. The day had begun in an almost summery warmth, but by mid afternoon it had become quite chilly and the aspect of the sky gave him some uneasiness. The sun had changed from blazing yellow into a duller orange and then to a listless globe of blood red. There would be fog. Already there was an acrid smell in the air;

the sky took on a brownish gloom which plunged the street into a sepia night. Then, quite distinctly, the clerk heard the basement door opening. Filled with a sense of enormous excitement, he waited until he heard the gentle squeal of the area gate, when he left his apartment pausing only to wrap a muffler round his neck to hide the awkward bruises. This time he was able to glimpse the old man and the child turning the corner into Green Lanes.

He ran lightly and rapidly after them, taking care to be as silent as they themselves; but when he reached Green Lanes he was confronted by a real blanket of brownish-yellow fog. His excitement was so high that this stroke of ill-luck almost unbalanced him. He cursed the fouled air violently, even absurdly shaking his fists at it. He was on the point of abandoning the pursuit when he heard the tell-tale sound of the phantom's hoop. It was extraordinarily plain and, in the absence of traffic noise—the fog had halted everything on wheels—he discovered he was able to follow it quite easily.

They could not have been much more than half a dozen yards ahead of him; so with lowered head and hand protectively before his face, he pursued the familiar tapping and rolling sound. He had not the slightest notion of where he was going as the dense air deprived him of all sense of distance and direction. However the unseen old man and child seemed to be keeping to the main roads; once he glimpsed an omnibus, gleaming with lamps, halted in a sea of dark air like some vessel becalmed and lost. Strained faces peered through the windows, and a shadowy driver comforted the uneasy horse. Then it all swirled away as the clerk hastened after the sound of the hoop.

Suddenly something uncanny fizzed and spat at his feet. He looked down and saw a fierce emission of sparks hissing on the pavement. He jumped away even as the sparks exploded with a sharp bang. There was a smell of gunpowder. He heard shrill laughter from close at hand.

Of course! he'd forgotten. It was November the Fifth. A child had thrown a firework at him. He glimpsed a ragged form and an impudently grinning face. He struck out, but the urchin had gone. He stumbled on in the wake of the phantom's hoop.

Several times he collided with mysterious passers by, and once with a lamp post; but the sound of the hoop was always just ahead. Then, quite abruptly, as if he'd burst through a doorway, he was out of the fog.

To his astonishment he discovered he was at the top of Ludgate Hill, directly facing St Paul's Cathedral. The Churchyard was quite deserted—save for the little ghost in its sailor's suit who stood upon the steps. Of Mr Fishbane there was no sign.

The child remained perfectly still, its hand on the hoop, like a figure in wax. The scene was so motionless and precise that the clerk was put in mind of the cabinet-maker's marvellous model. Helplessly he looked about him for the gigantic spectacles that would have transformed the huge domed building, the long street and even himself into an ingenious toy.

Then the child stirred and began to mount the remaining steps towards the pillared shadows of the entrance. "No!" breathed the clerk, suddenly aware of the horrible impropriety of a damned soul—even half a soul—entering such a place. Obsequiously he prayed that the little ghost would at least take off its hat . . .

The evening service was over. The mighty interior was dim and quiet. Two or three black gowned clerics moved among the seats and pillars like mice. Carved bishops lay against the walls on marble ottomans in which were stored their bones. Here and there grander tombs seemed to grow like brooding mushrooms in the shade of pale stone trees.

He saw the child, hat in hand, flicker from monument to monument as if reading the tablets on which multitudes of virtues were advertised in incomprehensible Latin.

The clerk started in alarm. A black gowned figure had approached the little boy. He heard the soft murmur of voices; he saw the cleric's smooth face crease in an indulgent

smile. They stood before the memorial to some sea-captain whose last heroic moments were represented in complicated stone. The child's eyes were wide; the clergyman was nodding. Doubtless he was asking the little boy in the sailor's suit if he too was going to be a sailor when he grew up.

Mr Fast smiled horribly. If only the clergyman knew what it was he was talking to, and whose dread hand the little boy had lately held . . .

He approached them. The priest looked up, and the pleasant smile on his face cooled. Bitterly the clerk realised he repelled the clergyman as much as the child had attracted him. It was a disagreeable fact he'd long tried to hide from himself but had never quite succeeded: people disliked him. He never knew why; he was clean and tidy, he was never pushing, he was careful to avoid giving offence, his breath was not unpleasant. Indeed, he often cupped his hands over his mouth to make sure. Yet for as long as he could remember people had avoided him whenever they decently could. Although the pain of this had long since lost its sharpness, he was suddenly aware of how bewilderingly unfair it was.

He lingered by a pillar. "I—I hope he's not troubling you . . . I hope he hasn't given offence . . ."

The priest—a young man still fresh in his office—shrugged his shoulders.

"How could a child do such a thing? He only wants a little affection, sir." He laid his hand very gently on the phantom's fair head.

The clerk suppressed a cry of agony and clutched at the pillar for support. It was as if fingers of iron had hammered on his own skull!

"I want everybody to love me," whispered the little ghost, and the cathedral was filled with the curious dry rustling of its voice. As it spoke it looked shyly from the clergyman to the dying hero on the wall and thence to the other stony sleepers who lay, it seemed, in clearings of a marble forest like some weird company of enchanted knights . . . "I want all the world to love me. I want people to smile and be glad to see me. I want them to make a space for me in all their hearts. I want them to honour and bless me. I want—"

"—And indeed they will!" smiled the clergyman.

"Liar!" moaned the clerk. "Liar—liar—liar!" His eyes were blazing with tears.

The priest glanced at him sharply, frowned, then turned back to the curious child whose longings had really moved him.

"Here, little boy—here's a sixpence for fireworks. And for a beginning to your dreams, I'll bless you gladly. And may all the rest follow."

He raised a little silver cross above the phantom's head.

"No!" screamed the clerk, appalled; he covered his head with his hands. His head was still racked by the agony of the touch of fingers; silver would have split his skull wide open.

He backed away; the priest stared at him as if he was mad. But the ghost, the ghost! An expression of unearthly fury had destroyed its childlike features.

"Bless me! Bless me!"

The clerk turned, and, with his head still hidden in his hands, fled out of the cathedral. He paused for a moment on the steps. The fog had filled up Ludgate Hill and was invading the Churchyard. It seemed to him that invisible hands were packing the whole gigantic structure in brown cotton wool for careful despatch. Already thick brown billows were being tucked round the statue of Queen Anne, and wisps of it were straying up the cathedral steps.

He heard the door behind him swing open; he fled down the wide stairway and back into the overwhelming fog. The memory of the ghost's fury terrified him. With outstretched arms he blundered down Ludgate Hill till his feet caught against a tangling piece of metal. He almost tripped, but succeeded in recovering himself. There was a violent crunching of glass and a sharp pain in his ankle as a splinter pierced through his trouser leg.

"My spectacles, Mr Fast! You've trodden on my spectacles!"

The voice sounded enormous and almost in his ear. It was the hateful, lisping voice of Mr Fishbane!

"Then stay blind!" screeched the clerk, and stumbled down Ludgate Hill to escape the evil old man and the child whose dreams and longed-for blessing would have smashed in his head.

Thank God for the fog! He continued blindly down the hill until he judged himself to be at Ludgate Circus; then he turned right to avoid any chance of coming unawares to the river. He stopped a moment—and heard nothing but the sighing of the troubled air. Then, very faintly, he heard the tap . . . tap . . . tap of a stick on an iron hoop. He trembled and hurried on; his situation was fearfully changed, from pursuer to pursued.

Or *was* it changed? Had he followed—or had he been led? Had the phantom been intent on destroying him from the very beginning? Was it, too—that pallid child in its sailor's suit—repelled by him, and had it so recoiled from what it was to become that it would blot him out?

He took several more turnings, to the left and the right and once almost into a house before he realised his mistake, in the hope of losing his pursuers. At times he could hear the distant swish and crackle of fireworks, followed by faint shouts of delight. Presently he glimpsed a vague glowing and flickering through the swirling fog; and there was a smell of smoke.

It was a bonfire. He must be passing some open space—though which one he'd no idea. Perhaps it was the consequence of some piece of demolition; he thought he saw a ragged wall . . . Something fizzed and roared and reddened the underside of huge billows in the air. He heard shrill laughter and screams and glimpsed high flames.

He halted; he could no longer hear the sound of the hoop. Slowly and filled with a strange apprehension he approached the fire. It was quite tremendous and as he drew near a black crowd seemed to grow out of the fog.

The great heat of the fire had cleared a space all round it; and urchins, like tattered imps, scampered hither and thither waving glowing fragments of wood and hurling them in the air so that there was a constant rain of sparks. The scene reminded him unpleasantly of the picture in Mr Fishbane's basement.

Obligingly the crowd made a space for him to observe the grandeur of the blaze, and eerily he recalled the phantom's words, "I want them to make a space for me . . ."

In the heart of the fire, tied onto a battered chair, was the effigy of Guy Fawkes—a crudely stuffed bundle of clothes with a painted face. Even as he watched, the figure, all robed in transparent veils of flame, began to topple; its arms fell back and its blazing head dropped from the broomstick that had supported it. The crowd shouted and cheered; and Mr Fast found himself joining them. He was ridiculously relieved to see that there *was* a broomstick underneath. The painted face, all crumpled by the intense heat, had seemed too like a tortured counterpart of his own.

Then Mr Fast saw the old man and the child. They were standing quite close to the flames. Mr Fishbane seemed to be smiling—a trifle critically, the clerk thought—as if he was used to superior conflagrations and more lively guys . . .

The phantom was staring at him. Its face, weirdly rosy in the glow, was once more contorted with fury. It raised its little hand and, with the hoop stick, pointed.

An urchin with a flaming brand scuttled by and tried to knock the stick aside. The glowing wood touched the phantom's hand. The clerk shrieked; his own flesh seemed to wither and char. He forced his way back through the crowd for the blessed sanctuary of the fog.

In moments the inferno was left behind him and once more he was in the blackish brown emptiness; the pain in his hand had diminished to a dull ache.

"Excuse me, sir—if you're not a lamp post or a pillarbox —may I stay with you? I don't know whether I'm on my

head or my heels. I'm quite lost—"

An old lady clutched at him, even hooked her umbrella round his arm.

"No!" snarled the clerk, not wanting to be hampered in his flight. He broke away, heedless of her cries of dismay and anxious apologies for having given offence. A moment later however, he repented; but the old lady had already vanished. He stopped and called softly; then, with a feeling of pleasure, he saw her again. She was turning round and round like an ungainly steeple cock, and holding out the crook of her umbrella.

"Excuse me, sir," she began; then recognising the disobliging clerk, begged his pardon for being so pushing again.

"Where are you going, ma'am?" he muttered awkwardly.

"To the station, sir. It's somewhere about here, I know—"

"Come," he said. "We'll try and find it together." He took her arm and began to walk while she unceasingly thanked him for his kindness.

Presently they fell in with other voyagers in the fog, most of whom were also searching for the station. At last they found it—a huge iron cathedral of wrought arches that soared and lost themselves in a high nothingness. Lamps hung, like misty suns in the coiling air; and a perfectly enormous clock face loomed out of nowhere as if some gigantic gentleman had produced it from a waistcoat pocket of unimaginable size, blackness and depth to dangle before some awestruck child.

Mr Fast supposed himself to be in Charing Cross Station. He was still holding the old lady's arm and so found himself at the ticket office. She bought a ticket to Chatham; and, with an abrupt thrill of excitement, the clerk bought one too. The unexpected prospect of a train journey filled him with an almost childish sense of hope and joy. The very smell of the place—the smoke, oil and coal—comforted him strangely; and the sounds of doors banging and steam escaping in loud sighs quickened his heart with a passionate dream of escape.

Evidently the old lady was glad of his company and together they went on to the platform where the train was waiting.

"Here's a carriage, young man." The old lady caught at his elbow with her umbrella crook. A door swung open and revealed a compartment filled with warm yellow light. Faces smiled out encouragingly at the new arrivals.

There is a comradeship in fog that is wonderfully hopeful. Every doubtful prospect is blotted out save the kindled warmth of companionship. People stumble upon one another out of a ghostly nothingness; smile answers smile and loneliness for a time is conquered . . .

"Come in—come in out of the cold. There's plenty of room."

It was plain they took the old lady to be a friend of his— even a relative. He felt almost proud of the connection even though it was only imaginary. He put his hand under her arm quite possessively.

Cheerfully the passengers made a space for the old lady and the clerk, even extending hands to help them in. There was a great air of rescue about it all and the clerk was sharply reminded of the phantom's longing words, "I want people to smile at me . . . to make a space for me . . ."

He settled himself by a window with suddenly moistened eyes. He glanced about him somewhat shyly. His fellow passengers seemed ordinary enough; they were lively and talkative and eager to exchange remarkable experiences in the fog. The old lady in particular was full of past terrors and was anxious to tell everyone of the young gentleman's extraordinary kindness without which, she felt sure, she'd be at the bottom of the river by now. Thus, for a time, Mr Fastfo. d him: the object of general approval and regard. Then it . ned (t that they'd all had similar adventures till it seemed that the whole foggy world had consisted of lost souls whose destiny had been to seek—and be found.

But the clerk could not quite join in; his own experience in the fog had been of too terrible a nature to be shared. He shrank to think how these good folk would stare at him if he confided the truth of his plight. He felt himself to be lost beyond all reach of ever being found.

"I think it's clearing a little," said a young man opposite who'd been industriously wiping the window and peering outside. " We should be moving soon."

It seemed he was in the confidence of the Railway Company, for soon after he gave his opinion, there came a piercing whistle followed by a loud gasp of steam as if the engine had been astonished by the astuteness of it. The train began to move.

The clerk stared through the window and observed the platform and the misty lights all slide away. He experienced an overwhelming feeling of relief. He turned with an eager smile to his companions in the compartment, suddenly ready to join with them in anything. They smiled back at him noddingly; but all their talk was spent. After all their alarms they were homeward bound; their eyes were filling up with dreams. Already the old lady, after a series of jerks and apologies for pushing her neighbour, had dozed off; her face was softly private with sleep. One by one the others followed, till only Mr Fast and the young man opposite remained awake.

But even the young man—though he could have been scarcely more than twenty—had the greatest difficulty in keeping his eyes open. The rocking of the carriage and the rattle of the wheels seemed to be a powerful lullaby.

"I'm afraid—" he mumbled, "you will be the—the last one—awake . . ." His eyelids drifted together, then opened briefly. He smiled sleepily. "To watch over us all." His voice sank to a whisper and then came the confused memory of a child's prayer. "Our souls to keep . . ."

He slept; and the clerk remained alone to guard sleepers from the terrors of the night.

Their heads leaned from side to side, as if they were co.

tinuing their animated chatter even through sleep. Mr Fast wondered if they shared each other's dreams—and if a semblance of himself was comfortably enrolled among them. Surely the old lady dreamed of her rescuer in the fog?

But it was the young man opposite who drew his gaze most often. His hands lay outstretched, with fingers gently opened. "Our souls to keep . . ."

A sudden swaying of the carriage huddled the sleepers closer together; the rattling of the wheels became momentarily uncertain. The clerk peered out of the window. At first he saw nothing but his own inquiring reflection and the tumbled heads and shoulders of the sleepers. He stared ahead and saw the front of the train entering on a bend in the line. He caught sight of the engine as it bored through the solid night under a tearing storm of smoke and sparks. Then, for no more than a second, as the curve became more acute, he saw the cabin of the engine—a fiery scarlet chapel in the blackness of the night. Then it vanished and he saw once more the reflection of his own face. It was stony with dread.

In the cabin, precisely outlined against the leaping flames, he had seen the phantom child! It was driving the train.

4 Although he'd almost certainly cried out at the shock, the sleepers had not wakened. Nor did they stir when, some ten minutes after, the train drew in at a small country station, the name of which drifted by as a meaningless jumble of letters.

Silently the clerk climbed out of the compartment and onto the platform. He stared towards the tremendous green and gold engine with its wheels like stupendous iron hoops; clouds of steam kept obscuring it so that it seemed to be floating in a turbulent white sea. The guard whistled and the train began to move. Painfully Mr Fast watched the bright warm compartment roll away out of his life. "Our souls to keep," he murmured. "Our souls to keep."

The platform filled with billowing gusts of smoke into which the train vanished with a loud sigh. By the time the air had cleared the lights on the last carriage had dwindled to pinpricks.

He stared up and down the platform, expecting to see the terrible little ghost standing there, glaring at him. But the platform was deserted. He walked away and left his ticket at the barrier. At every step he paused, waiting to hear the tap . . . tap . . . tap of the phantom's hoop. But there was nothing; only the sighing of the night and the creaking of the ticket-collector's gate.

"Cab, sir?"

An old fashioned cab was standing outside the station; it was tall, dark and excessively narrow—as was the melancholy horse that loitered between the shafts. Having nowhere to go, nor even knowing where he was, Mr Fast shrugged his shoulders and climbed into the cab.

Within there was a curious smell that was vaguely familiar, although, for a moment the clerk could not place it.

"Where to, Mr Fast?"

The driver's hatch had snapped open—and the hateful face of Mr Fishbane peered down! The clerk screamed feebly, as might some small trapped animal, in pathetic defiance.

"Why are you here?"

"It's a living, Mr Fast. But it's more for the occupation than the profit."

"Where is he?"

"D'you mean Dennis? I thought you saw him. It's what he always wanted, you know, to be an engine driver. I understand he told you. You ought to be happy for him. It's all very well for you and me to smile over a child's dreams and ambitions, but there's a rare grandness to them that makes the old heart ache. Don't it make you sigh to think of him rushing through the night, bound for—"

"—hell!" whispered the clerk, burying his face in his hands as if to shut out his thoughts.

"Chatham," corrected the old man reproachfully. "Maybe not the loveliest spot in the world, but certainly not to be compared with where you mentioned. You're too full of fancies, my friend. You must have been a very fanciful child. What am I saying? We *know* you were a fanciful child, don't we!"

The old man chuckled at his stroke of humour; but the clerk was seized with a fit of feverish trembling that rocked the cab. He could not get it out of his mind that the phantom child was fixed on destroying him—and, believing him to be still on the train, was driving it to destruction. He thought of the bright compartment with its warm nest of sleepers . . .

"They'll be killed—all of them . . . even in their sleep."

There was a moment's silence. The old man's face, peering down through the hatch, seemed curiously softened. His rheumy eyes blinked like vague stars—and the clerk was caught in them as might be a child under the roof of heaven. His dread began to tilt towards awe . . .

"Let me take you to an inn for the night," murmured Mr Fishbane, breaking the spell as if by design. "You're a rich man, Mr Fast. Let me drive you somewhere charming. By the sea, perhaps? Or do you care for mountains? Very bracing, I understand. Anywhere you like, Mr Fast; you name it, and I'll oblige."

"The train—the train!"

"What about Harrogate or Bath—or even Brighton?"

"They trusted me—the people in the compartment; even asked me to keep their souls—"

"Souls, souls, souls! How much do they weigh apiece? Do you pay tax on 'em? Do you keep 'em on the public highway? Come, come, Mr Fast! You're talking nonsense! Where shall I drive you?"

"Take everything back! Take all my soul—only stop the train!"

"No more bargains, Mr Fast. That Contract of yours was a real tangle, my friend. Not even a fly could have got through the knots you tied. What chance would a bulky old fellow like me have?"

The clerk raised his face to the opened hatch with such a look of anguish and despair that the old man was forced to blink and look away a moment.

"All right, Mr Fishbane. Let there be no bargain . . . only keep your word. You said you would take me anywhere. Take me to the train before it's too late."

"A gloomy choice, Mr Fast. Are you sure?"

The clerk nodded. The necessity of his choice filled him, not with dread but with an inexplicable tenderness. The sleeping passengers in the doomed compartment seemed to him to be the most precious things in the universe. Had he but wakened them before he'd crept out like a thief, then perhaps . . .? Certainly it was the thought of their sleeping that was hardest of all to bear; and the memory of the young man with his hands outstretched in a gesture of trust and the child's prayer still warm on his lips, sent an arrow of pain through the clerk's heart. He closed his eyes, thereby exchanging one darkness for another.

"Come, Mr Fast. A last chance. Let me drive you somewhere bright and cheerful?" The old man's voice was wheedling and cajoling. He seemed really concerned. "It seems a real shame to throw yourself away like this."

"Stop mocking me, Mr Fishbane. I'm near the end of my journey. Let me finish it in my own fashion."

The old man sighed and gently shook his head. The hatch snapped shut and the clerk heard the whip crackle. The cab jolted into motion and there was a sound of hooves slipping and scrambling over cobbles. In a few moments the movement of the cab became regular and the chief sounds were the queer cries of Mr Fishbane to his horse, urging it on.

It did not seem as if they were travelling very rapidly, but when the clerk glanced through the window he was amazed at the pace at which the hedgerows sped past. He caught distant glimpses of brightly lit houses, and even of mansions, which were extinguished almost as soon as he saw them. Then a church fled by, and he'd an aching longing to go inside it; till a policeman, about some ferocious business of the law, glared in angry amazement at the unforeseen cab—and left his stern image printed on the clerk's inner eye. They passed what looked to be a ruined abbey, all gnawed and

ragged to the night, and a graveyard tottering round it, so
that it seemed all the houses, the church and even the policeman had been shovelled, pell-mell, into this quiet oblivion.

Now the cab began to jolt and jump, as if they had turned
off the road and were galloping across fields. For seconds the
wheels seemed to leave the ground altogether; and at one
point they flew past a man on horseback who looked
frightened and half held out a hand as if to help the white-
faced traveller in the hurtling cab.

Then trees and houses and more houses were born only to
perish at once; a crossroads rushed by, but no man could
have told what was written on the signpost's bony arms.
And all the while the clerk clung fiercely to a strap to save
himself from being flung out into the racing air.

"The train, Mr Fast."

They had stopped. The hatch opened and Mr Fishbane was looking in as if surprised to find his passenger still whole and alive. The clerk climbed out. They were poised on the ridge of an embankment below which glinted the railway line, like a huge iron snake filletted by the worms of the night.

Mr Fast looked up at his coachman. The old man, perched on the driver's seat, his shabby coat hanging down like folded wings, looked more like a disreputable vulture than ever.

"The train, Mr Fast."

Very faintly he heard the rattle of wheels. He stared along the line but could see nothing by reason of a bend that skirted a low, wooded hill. He fell on his knees beside the cab, holding onto the door handle for support as the ground was treacherous and steep.

"Stop it, Mr Fishbane. Please . . ."

"I'm an old man, Mr Fast. What could I do with such a rushing, heavy thing?"

Already white smoke was lifting up above the distant trees, and the rattling of the wheels was becoming louder. The rails began to quiver and shudder until it seemed no longer possible that their rivets would hold. Shadows turned to gaps; the line seemed to be crumbling before the clerk's very eyes.

This was where the train would be destroyed. He had been brought to see it. The night seemed filled with the frightful, grinding crash, the wild screams—and then the appalling silence of nothingness. In his mind's eye, he saw the mountainous wreckage, rearing up like an iron cathedral, filled with tangled tombs. He saw himself wandering beside it until he came to the place he sought. A jagged, twisted window through which protruded a young man's hands, still outstretched in their gesture of trust. They were bright with blood . . .

"You can stop it—you must stop it!"

He rose to his feet and tried to drag the old man from his

perch. He might as well have tried to pull down a mountain.

"Too old, Mr Fast. Old limbs ain't made for running. An old voice too feeble to be heard."

"Devil!" shrieked the clerk, abandoning his futile efforts to drag the old man down.

"After all I've done for you, Mr Fast? Where's your gratitude? You're on your own, Mr Fast. You should be proud. You're a free agent," said the old man coolly, and straightened his crumpled coat. "Don't you understand, my friend, you're alone?"

"Alone?"

It was possible that the old man might have answered this last question, but it was too late as the clerk had already begun to scramble down the steep embankment.

He leaped and fell and rolled and struggled up again like a child in the very ecstasy of flight. At times he felt himself to be winged and was almost angry to feel his feet strike heavily on the ground. At last he reached the bottom; he looked back half defiantly to the line of the embankment against the sky. He thought he saw an arm wave to him; then the thunderous roar of the train overwhelmed him.

"Dennis—Dennis!" he screamed as the monstrous engine rushed round the bend. He stumbled towards it, catching his feet against the wooden sleepers and waving his arms and shouting. But his voice was lost in the terrific uproar. He saw the engine's buffers coming at him like enormous iron fists; he saw the mighty smoke stack belching speckled fire —and beyond it, like an implacable red eye, he saw the cabin window against which was pressed the joyful face of the phantom child. He cried out again—but he and his voice were whirled away into the shaking night.

The train halted some little way beyond the place of the tragedy. The engine driver and fireman were the first to alight. They were much shaken and anxious to assure the guard and the gathering crowd of passengers that there was

nothing they could have done. The gentleman had rushed so suddenly onto the track that there'd been no chance at all of stopping in time. He'd been carried forward on the buffers and only fallen to the side of the line when the train had stopped.

Lights were fetched and the guard—who, while yielding to the driver when the train was in motion, took full command when it wasn't—set about searching the stranger's clothing. Then an old lady who'd been in a compartment near the rear of the train, cried out in surprise and distress. She recognised the stranger as the kindly young man who'd helped her in the fog near Charing Cross and had actually travelled some little way with her. She'd thought he was going all the way to Chatham and had no idea when he'd got off as she'd fallen asleep. This puzzled the guard greatly and he regretted his assumption of authority as, in the circumstances, he did not quite know what to do with it. The knotty problem of an unexpended portion of ticket raised its head, so he was inclined to doubt the old lady's word. Then others from the same compartment confirmed it; they were all deeply distressed as the stranger had seemed so gentle and amiable a soul. Indeed, they went so far as to declare they'd never forget him. Such real gentlemen were all too rare nowadays. There had been an instinctive warmth about him, so that one would have been glad to have him for a friend. "I dreamed about him," said a young man rather awkwardly. "But all I can remember was that he seemed to be very happy."

However, none of this contributed to solving the guard's predicament which had worsened by his failure to find the stranger's ticket.

"I'll have to make a report to the Company," he muttered gloomily, "and I don't know what they'll say to it." He stood back with the air of leaving the matter in abeyance in case the Company decided against its having happened at all.

It was then that a curious and even disquieting thing

happened. A little boy in an old-fashioned sailor's suit seemed to have appeared from nowhere at all and was kneeling beside the poor man's head which he cradled in his pale hands. No one could recall having seen this child anywhere on the train, but there was no doubt he was closely connected with the dead man. With horrified sympathy the crowd moved back. Those nearest thought they heard the child whisper something, and the fireman could have sworn he heard the words, "My son . . . oh my son . . ." But as this made no sort of sense, the man being old enough to be the child's father instead of the other way round, he concluded he'd imagined it or the man had, at that moment, been still alive.

Meaning to comfort the child and perhaps draw him away, the fireman moved forward; but as he did so he found himself gently but firmly pushed aside by a shabby old man in black who shook his head and smiled and took the child by the hand.

It was all so utterly unexpected—and the night scene itself, with the clustering oil lamps flickering on the brasswork of the huge panting engine and on the intent crowd gazing down on the shattered gentleman on the track, was so very strange and unearthly—that the fireman could do nothing but stare.

"Come, Dennis," murmured the old man. "Come away, my dear."

Then this weird pair—the shabby old man and the little boy in the sailor's suit—drifted away from the glowing scene and seemed to mount the embankment and so dissolve in the upper reaches of the night.

"Where shall we go now?" whispered the little phantom, its pale face smiling up into the old man's.

"God knows," answered Mr Fishbane; and his beard streamed out to catch the stars.